Why Do Dogs Bark?

by JOAN HOLUB

illustrations by Anna DiVito

PUFFIN BOOKS

PUFFIN BOOKS
Published by the Penguin Group
Penguin Putnam Books for Young Readers, 345 Hudson Street, New York, New York 10014, U.S.A.
Penguin Books Ltd, 27 Wrights Lane, London W8 5TZ, England
Penguin Books Australia Ltd, Ringwood, Victoria, Australia
Penguin Books Canada Ltd, 10 Alcorn Avenue, Toronto, Ontario, Canada M4V 3B2
Penguin Books (N.Z.) Ltd, 182-190 Wairau Road, Auckland 10, New Zealand

Penguin Books Ltd, Registered Offices: Harmondsworth, Middlesex, England

First published by Dial Books for Young Readers and Puffin Books,
divisions of Penguin Putnam Books for Young Readers, 2001

3 5 7 9 10 8 6 4 2

THE LIBRARY OF CONGRESS HAS CATALOGED THE DIAL EDITON AS FOLLOWS:
Holub, Joan.
Why do dogs bark? / by Joan Holub.
p.   cm.
Summary: Questions and answers present information about the origins, behavior,
and characteristics of dogs and their interaction with humans.
ISBN 0-8037-2504-3 (hardcover)
1. Dogs—Behavior—Miscellanea—Juvenile literature. 2. Dogs—Miscellanea—Juvenile literature.
[1. Dogs—Miscellanea. 2. Questions and answers.] I. Title.
SF433.H68 2001 636.7—dc21 00-023984

Puffin Books ISBN 0-14-056789-5
Puffin® and Easy-to-Read® are registered trademarks of Penguin Putnam Inc.

Printed in U.S.A.
Set in ITC Century Book

Reading Level 2.4

Photo Credits

Front cover; pages 7, 9 (Australian Shepherd, Mixed Breed and Boston Terrier),
25, 33, 45 copyright © Davis/Lynn Images
Pages 1, 5 (Golden Retriever), 10, 11, 14 (two wolves–D.Robert Franz), 15 (Rita
Summers), 18, 21, 23, 36, 37, 38, 39, 48 copyright © Ron Kimball Studios
Pages 13, 34 copyright © Elizabeth Hathon

With thanks to Joy and Dena,
my wonderful editors

Thanks to Stephen Zawistowski, PH.D.,
Certified Applied Animal Behaviorist, for his help—J.H.

For Michael and Stephen Olinger—A.D.

Do you love dogs?

Many people love dogs.

Dogs are even called "man's best friend."

There are over one hundred kinds,

or breeds, of pet dogs.

Some popular breeds are retrievers,
cocker spaniels, poodles, beagles,
Rottweilers (ROT-wy-lerz),
and German shepherds.
Dogs that are a mix of breeds
are called mixed-breeds or mutts.

Which dogs are smallest and biggest?

Dogs come in many different shapes and sizes.

Chihuahuas (chuh-WAH-waz) are the smallest dogs.

A Teacup Chihuahua will fit in your hand.

Mastiffs and Saint Bernards are the biggest dogs.

They can weigh over 250 pounds.

That is about as much as four kids your age!

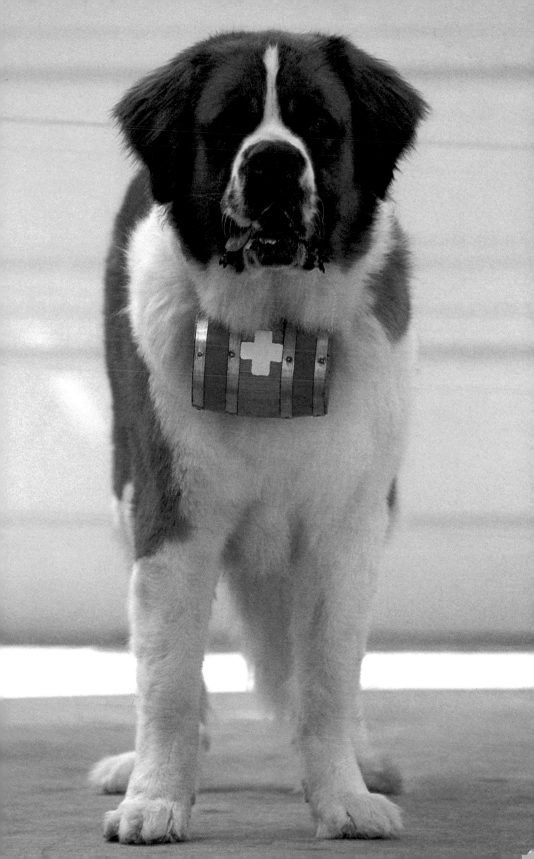

Which dogs are best?

No one breed of dog is best

at everything.

But many breeds have special skills.

Greyhounds can run very fast.

They have powerful legs and thin bodies.

Some can run forty miles an hour.

Terriers (TER-ee-urz) are brave.

They will hunt animals that are

much larger than they are.

Retrievers (ree-TREE-vurz) are

great swimmers.

They have webbed toes

to help them swim.

They can even swim underwater.

What can your dog do best?

How many puppies can a dog have at one time?

A group of puppies born at one time
is called a litter.

A mother dog can have many puppies
in one litter.

Five is the most common number.

One dog had a litter
of twenty-two puppies!
Newborn puppies of all breeds
look a lot alike.
It can be hard to tell what breed
a newborn puppy is.

How does a puppy grow up to be a dog?

Puppies are born with their eyes closed.
They can't see or hear until they are
two to three weeks old.
When puppies are three to four weeks
old, they begin to walk, bark, play,
and wag their tails.

Puppies drink milk from their mothers

until they are five to seven weeks old.

They may also lick their mother's face,

so she'll spit up food for them to eat.

Then they are usually ready

to eat puppy food.

Most puppies become full-grown dogs

when they are one year old.

Are dogs related to wolves?

Yes! A long time ago, there were no dogs.

Then people taught some wolves

to be helpful.

Over hundreds of years, some of these

wolves changed.

They became the dogs we have today.

Other wolves did not change.

They are still wild.

What is a pack of dogs or wolves?

A pack is like a dog's family.

Dogs and wolves like to eat, play,

and sleep with their pack.

Each pack has one leader.

Your dog thinks your family is its pack.

It thinks someone in your family

is the leader.

Do you know who?

Why do dogs bark?

Your dog barks to protect your house
and yard.

When a stranger comes around,

it barks to sound an alarm.

It wants to tell you and your family

that a stranger is nearby.

Your dog may also bark to tell a stranger to go away.

Some dogs bark to greet their owners when they come home.

Why do dogs howl?

Some dogs howl when they are lonely.
If your dog is alone for too long,
it may howl.
It is trying to find you or
its dog friends.
Other dogs may howl
back to say hello.

Some dogs howl when they hear singing,
music, or sirens.

They think it sounds like other dogs
howling, so they want to howl back.

Why do dogs bury bones?

Dogs and wolves almost always
want to eat.
Wolves must work hard to find food.
They eat fast, before other animals
can steal their food.
That is where the saying "wolf it down"
comes from.
When wolves have extra food,
they bury it to save it for later.

Pet dogs also worry that someone
will take their food.
So they eat fast too.
Some pet dogs bury or hide bones
to save them for later.
Does your dog do this?

Can dogs see better than people?

Dogs can see better than people can at night.

They are also better at seeing movement from far away.

But dogs do not see colors very well.

They can see the color blue.

But most other colors look gray to a dog.

Can dogs hear better than people?

Yes! Dogs can hear high tones and soft sounds that people can't hear. You can't hear the high sound of a dog whistle, but your dog can. Dogs can also tell which direction a sound is coming from better than you can.

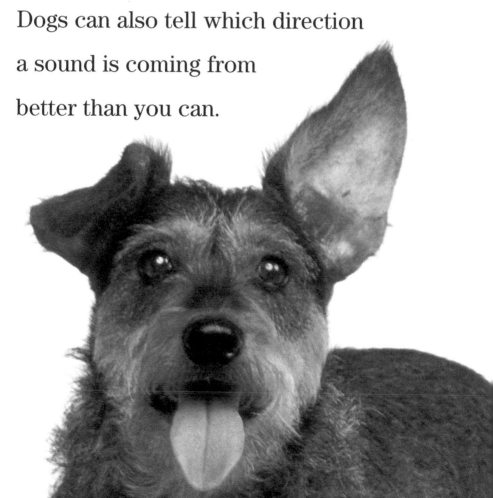

Why do dogs sniff you?

Smell is a dog's most important sense.

A dog's sense of smell is over one

hundred times better than your

sense of smell.

A dog sniffs you to find out who you are.

It can probably tell if you are afraid

by how you smell too.

Does your dog sniff you?

Your dog remembers how you smell

better than it remembers what you

look like.

Why do dogs lick people?

Dogs smell through their noses.

They also smell through

very tiny openings in their mouths

behind their top front teeth.

Licking can help dogs find out

who people and other dogs are.

Dogs may also lick people because

they like the taste of their salty skin.

Why do dogs pee so often on a walk?

Dogs pee to leave their own special smell behind.

They want other dogs to know they were there.

They are also saying, "This place is mine!"

Why do dogs roll in stinky stuff?

Dogs sometimes like to roll

in other animals' poop or in garbage.

They do this to cover their own smell.

In the wild, some animals run away

if they smell a dog or wolf nearby.

Dogs and wolves cover their smell

so they can sneak up on other animals.

Why do dogs pant?

When a dog pants, it breathes hard

and fast through its open mouth.

Dogs pant when they are too hot.

It helps them cool off.

People sweat to cool off.

But dogs cannot sweat through their fur.

They lose heat through their

tongues instead.

Why do dogs have bad breath?

Over time, slime forms on a dog's

teeth and gums.

This can smell bad.

Dogs can't brush their teeth.

Wouldn't you have bad breath

if you never brushed?

Why do dogs wag their tails?

Dogs wag their tails when they
are happy.

If a dog's tail is down between its
back legs, it is scared or unhappy.

When two dogs meet, their tails show
what they are thinking.

If their tails stick out straight,
they are deciding who is in charge.

If one dog's tail is high and the other's
is low, the high-tail dog is the boss.

What other ways do dogs talk with their bodies?

Your dog uses its body to show how it feels and to tell you what it wants. When your dog rolls onto its back, it may be saying "You are the boss" or "Rub my tummy." If its tail and ears stand straight up and it shows its teeth, your dog is angry.

When your dog holds out one paw,

it is asking you for something.

If your dog bows down on its front legs,

that usually means it wants to play.

What kinds of jobs can dogs do?

Your dog's job is to be your friend.

But dogs can do many other jobs.

Some bloodhounds help find lost people.

Their keen sense of smell also helps

them track criminals.

Sheepdogs and collies can herd.
They are good at rounding up sheep
or cows.
Some huskies pull snowsleds.
They have thick, warm fur
and lots of energy.
Some German shepherds are trained
to be Seeing Eye dogs or police dogs.
They are fast learners, very smart,
and good at obeying directions.

What other kinds of jobs can dogs do?

Saint Bernards are good at finding

people lost in snowstorms.

They have a very strong sense of smell.

They can also sense the body heat of

a person buried under snow.

Doberman Pinschers (DO-ber-mun PIN-

sherz) can be guard dogs.

They will bark to scare away strangers.

Some dogs are actors.

They are good at following directions

and staying calm.

They do not get upset by

the lights and noise on

a television or movie set.

Are any dogs heroes?

Balto

Many dogs have done brave things.

A sled dog named Balto once helped

carry medicine to a town in Alaska.

He ran for twenty hours in a snowstorm.

Without his help, many people

would have died.

Barry

A Saint Bernard named Barry

rescued many people

lost in snowstorms.

He once saved a small girl

who was buried in the snow.

He lay down next to her

to keep her warm.

Then he pulled her to a nearby house.

Buddy

A German shepherd named Buddy

was the first Seeing Eye dog.

Buddy was trained to help a blind man.

Buddy helped him cross streets safely.

For the first time, the man could

travel and go to work on his own,

thanks to Buddy.

Do dogs understand words?

Experts think some dogs can learn

twenty or more words.

This helps make dogs easier

to train than many other animals.

Most dogs can learn the command words

sit, stay, and *come.*

Dogs may understand many other words.

How many words does your dog know?

good dog

Training

When your dog is old enough,

you can teach it to obey and do tricks.

Train your dog for only

one to five minutes each time.

Teach one trick at a time.

Speak slowly and clearly.

Never hit or shout at your dog.

Always say "good dog" and give your dog

a treat, a hug, or a pat when it obeys.

Training your dog to sit

Hold a small treat over your dog's nose.

Move the treat backward

over your dog's head.

Gently push your dog's rear down

until it sits.

Each time your dog sits down,

say "sit," and give it the treat.

Training your dog to come

Stand about five steps away
from your dog.

Look into its eyes for a moment.

Then say "come."

Use hand movements, too.

Try to teach your dog to sit instead of
jumping up when it comes to you.

come

Training your dog to stay

Hold one hand out with your palm

facing your dog.

Say "stay."

Keep your hand out.

Step away from your dog slowly

and say "stay" over and over.

If your dog does not stay put, start again.

Most pet dogs want to be

their owner's best buddy.

Your dog loves you.

Take good care of your dog . . .

and it will be your friend forever.

Why Do Cats Meow?

by JOAN HOLUB

illustrations by Anna DiVito

PUFFIN BOOKS

PUFFIN BOOKS
Published by the Penguin Group
Penguin Putnam Books for Young Readers, 345 Hudson Street, New York, New York 10014, U.S.A.
Penguin Books Ltd, 27 Wrights Lane, London W8 5TZ, England
Penguin Books Australia Ltd, Ringwood, Victoria, Australia
Penguin Books Canada Ltd, 10 Alcorn Avenue, Toronto, Ontario, Canada M4V 3B2
Penguin Books (N.Z.) Ltd, 182-190 Wairau Road, Auckland 10, New Zealand

Penguin Books Ltd, Registered Offices: Harmondsworth, Middlesex, England

First published by Dial Books for Young Readers and Puffin Books,
divisions of Penguin Putnam Books for Young Readers, 2001

1 3 5 7 9 10 8 6 4 2

Text copyright © Joan Holub, 2001
Illustrations copyright © Anna DiVito, 2001
All rights reserved

THE LIBRARY OF CONGRESS HAS CATALOGED THE DIAL EDITION AS FOLLOWS:
Holub, Joan.
Why do cats meow? / Joan Holub.
p. cm.
Summary: Questions and answers present information about the history, behavior,
and characteristics of cats and their interaction with humans.
ISBN 0-8037-2503-5 (hardcover)
1. Cats—Behavior—Miscellanea—Juvenile literature. 2. Cats—Miscellanea—Juvenile literature.
[1. Cats—Miscellanea. 2. Questions and answers.] I. Title.
SF446.5.H66 2001 636.8—dc21 00-023985

Puffin Books ISBN 0-14-056788-7
Puffin® and Easy-to-Read® are registered trademarks of Penguin Putnam Inc.

Printed in U.S.A.

Reading Level 2.3

Photo Credits

Front cover; pages 1, 9, 14, 16, 20, 22, 23 (gray cat and cheetah),
26, 27, 29, 30, 32, 35, 42 copyright © Ron Kimball Studios
Page 8 copyright © Nancy Sheehan
Pages 13, 23 (orange cat), 37, 39 copyright © Davis/Lynn Images

*With thanks to Joy and Dena,
my wonderful editors*

*Thanks to Stephen Zawistowski, PH.D.,
Certified Applied Animal Behaviorist, for his help*—J.H.

For Ann, Diane, and Justin—A.D.

Do you love cats?

Many people love cats.

Cats are the most popular pet

in the United States.

Dogs are second.

Cats are good buddies.

Most pet cats are cuddly, playful,

and loving.

How big is the biggest cat?

One pet cat is on record weighing a whopping forty-seven pounds! That's as much as a six-year-old child might weigh.

But most pet cats are much smaller. They weigh about six to eighteen pounds.

How much does your cat weigh?

Here is how you can find out:

Weigh yourself.

Hold your cat and weigh yourself again.

Subtract the first number

from the second.

Now you know how much

your cat weighs!

How small is a newborn kitten?

A newborn kitten is so tiny

that it will fit in your hand.

It only weighs about three or four ounces.

When kittens are born, they can't see

or hear.

A kitten's eyes open after a week or so.
It can leave its mother when it is eight
to twelve weeks old.
By the time it is six months old, a kitten
can hunt and take care of itself.

How many kittens can a cat have?

A mother cat usually has two to five kittens at one time.

She could have more than twenty kittens a year.

One cat had four hundred kittens in her lifetime!

Kittens are fun.

But it can be hard to find homes

for so many kittens.

Why do cats meow?

When your cat meows, it could mean
many things.

A soft meow or chirp may be
your cat's way of saying hello.

A loud, long meow means that your cat
wants something.

It may be hungry.

Maybe it wants to play or go outside.

Listen to your cat's different meows.

Try to guess what each one means.

Why do cats purr?

A purr is the soft rumbling sound a cat makes.

Kittens purr when they are nursing.

Cats may purr if they are happy.

Did you know that cats may also purr if they are upset?

Purring makes them feel better.

Pet your cat for a few minutes.

Can you hear it purr?

Why do cats hiss?

Cats hiss when they are mad or afraid.

When a cat hisses, it may also spit,

arch its back, and puff out its fur.

It is trying to look big and scary

to frighten an enemy.

Watch out!

Hissing may mean a cat is ready

to scratch or bite.

Can cats see in the dark?

Cats can see much better than people
can at night.

But they can't see in total darkness.

The back part of a cat's eyes reflects
light like a mirror.

This helps it see with only a tiny bit
of light.

It also makes a cat's eyes glow
in the dark.

In darkness the pupil in the center

of a cat's eye opens wide.

This lets in as much light as possible

to help the cat see better.

Look at your eyes in a mirror.

Do the pupils in your eyes get bigger

in low light too?

Can cats hear sounds that people can't hear?

Does your cat ever act like it hears something—when you don't hear anything?

Cats can hear very high sounds,

such as mouse squeaks,

that people and dogs cannot hear.

A cat's ears turn to listen for

danger sounds.

What is the difference between wild cats and pet cats?

Lions, tigers, and leopards are all wild cats.

Pet cats and wild cats have a lot in common.

They both like to hunt.

They both like to spend time alone.

They both like to play.

But there are many differences too.

Wild cats are usually bigger than pet cats.

They live in jungles and forests.

They do not trust people.

Your cat learned to trust people when it

was a kitten.

Why do pet cats hunt?

Wild cats hunt for food.

But pet cats like to hunt even if they are fed by people.

Mother cats teach their kittens to hunt by bringing mice and birds to them.

If your cat brings a mouse or bird

to you, don't get mad.

Your cat is giving you a present

to help you learn to hunt and

to show it loves you.

Just ask your parents to bury your

cat's gift.

Why do cats have claws?

Cats have five toes on each front paw
and four toes on each back paw.
One claw is hidden in each toe.
Cats can slide their claws out when they
need them.
They use their claws to climb, hunt,
or fight.

Why do cats scratch?

Cats sometimes scratch furniture to

sharpen their claws.

They scratch marks on trees to tell

other cats they have been there.

Cats may scratch other animals

if they get scared.

Never pull a cat's tail or play too rough.

The cat won't like it and may

scratch you!

Why do cats have whiskers?

Cat whiskers are thick, stiff hairs.

A cat has about twelve whiskers

on each side of its face.

If it loses a whisker, it can grow a

new one.

Its whiskers grow a little longer than its
body is wide.
When a cat pokes its head into
a small space, its whiskers tell it if the
rest of its body will fit.
Whiskers also help cats find their way
in the dark.

Why do cats have tails?

People hold out their arms to keep

their balance when they walk

on a balance beam.

A cat uses its tail in the same way.

It moves its tail back and forth

to help keep its balance.

When a cat holds its tail high,

it is probably happy.

If its tail droops down, it is unháppy

or scared.

If the tip of its tail waves very quickly,

your cat may be ready to pounce!

How much do cats sleep?

Cats sleep about sixteen hours a day.

They are only awake for eight hours!

How many hours do you sleep?

Cats take lots of short naps,

called catnaps.

Does your cat ever twitch while it

is sleeping?

This could mean it is dreaming.

What do you think your cat

dreams about?

Do cats need baths?

Most cats don't like to get wet.
So they won't like it if you give
them a bath.
But cats usually don't need baths.
They lick their fur to get clean.
A cat's tongue feels rough,
like sandpaper.

Try to lick your ear.

You can't, can you?

Cats can't lick their ears either.

They wash their ears by licking

a front paw and rubbing it

behind each ear.

Why does your cat like to rub against you?

Cats do this because it feels good.

They are also rubbing their cat smell

on you.

People can't smell this cat smell—

but other cats can.

Your cat is telling them that it owns you.

So they had better stay away!

Why do cats like to be petted?

Most cats like to be petted because
it feels good.

Mother cats lick their kittens to smooth
their fur.

When you pet your cat, it reminds your
cat of being licked by its mother.

Why do cats go in and out so much?

Your cat thinks it owns your house
and yard.
An indoor cat patrols the rooms
in a house.
It watches cats and birds
through the windows.

An outdoor cat likes to go outside
to see if anything has changed.
It checks to see if other cats have
visited and left their cat smell.
It will also rub against trees and fences
to leave its own cat smell behind.
Then it likes to come back inside
where it is safe and cozy.

Are there any cat heroes?

Scarlett

A mother cat named Scarlett was
very brave.

She lived in an empty building
with her five kittens.

One day the building caught on fire.

Scarlett carried her kittens outside,
one by one.

She risked her life to save her kittens.

There was danger each time she carried
a kitten from the fire.

Zowie

Zowie is a cat that visits people
who are lonely or sick.
Zowie is very brave.
She is not afraid of loud noises or
moving wheelchairs.
Zowie stays calm when strangers
pet her.
When Zowie comes for a visit,
she makes people smile.

What toys do cats like?

Does your cat chase your pencil when you write or draw?

Cats like to play with things that move. They are pretending to hunt, just like wild cats!

Boing! Boing!

A Ping-Pong ball makes a great cat toy.

Draw a picture on one to make

it special.

Use a marker that is child-safe

and will not rub off.

Roll the ball down a long hall

and watch your cat go!

Ssssnake!

Get a long piece of string.

You can tie a ribbon or paper bow

to the end for extra fun.

Wiggle the string snake.

Pull it behind you as you walk.

Watch your cat hunt the snake.

Fishing pole

Tie a string to one end of a stick.

Tie the other end of the string to a small

foam or newspaper ball.

Now go fishing!

Dangle the ball in front of your cat.

Swish it around.

Watch your cat chase the ball.

Kitty condo

Find a large box and ask an adult
to cut different-size holes in it.
Decorate the box so it looks like
a house for your cat.
You can also add cat pictures, your cat's
name, and paw prints.
Watch your cat have fun going in and
out of the holes.

Catnip mouse

Draw a mouse face on the toe

of an old white sock.

Pour a little catnip into the sock.

Tie a knot in the top of the sock.

Let your cat sniff it.

Some cats act silly when they

smell catnip.

Does yours?

Cats may act like they can take care
of themselves.

But cats need people to help take care
of them.

Your cat loves you and needs you . . .

and it wants you to love it back.